D0688474

## For Tom,
## il mio amore

First edition 2005

Library of Congress Cataloging-in-Publication Data is available.

Library of Congress Catalog Card Number 2004062873

ISBN 0-7636-2396-2

1 2 3 4 5 6 7 8 9 10

Printed in China

This book was typeset in Maiandra.
The illustrations were done in gouache, watercolor, crayon, and pen.

Candlewick Press
2067 Massachusetts Avenue
Cambridge, Massachusetts 02140

visit us at www.candlewick.com

# Pino and the
# Signora's Pasta

## Janet Pedersen

CANDLEWICK PRESS
CAMBRIDGE, MASSACHUSETTS

The cats waited.
They waited under the last
golden rays of the Roman sun.
They nipped at each other,
they scowled, they howled.
The cats were waiting . . .
waiting only for the Signora.

Finally, the sweet steamy aroma
came drifting through the courtyard
to greet every whiskered nose.
The Signora had arrived!

"No mangia tonight, sweet Pino?"
asked the Signora. "Why, you
were once a sad and purr-less
kitty, the size of a cannoli.
Now look how grande
you've become! Come, gatto.
The moon will be full tonight.
You should be too.
Mangia, Pino, mangia!"

"Pasta, pasta, pasta!
I'm tired of pasta.
I'm bored with pasta!" said Pino.
"Couldn't the Signora bring a
tasty chop? A delicious fish?
Perhaps a nice stew?
A special meal is
what I want!"

Soon the courtyard filled with the musical purring
that comes only after a meal of the Signora's pasta.

Pino, Pino,
don't you know?
The Signora loves you so!
Mangia, mangia, take a bite....
Purrrrr to your heart's delight!

Purr

Purr

Purr

Purr

Purr

"Basta pasta!" Pino said.
"I will find a better meal tonight—
one that will make me purr
as loud as a lion!"

Pino arrived at an outdoor café.

"Bellissimo! What have we here?
A fine fish that tastes so fresh—
I can almost feel it jumping in
my tummy! I must order another
platter so I can purr like the
best-fed cat in all of Rome!"

Chomp
Chomp
Chomp

# "Shooo, cat! Shoooo!"

yelled the waiter.

So Pino moved on.

"Ah! Golden crusts! Perhaps if I sit here a bit longer, a more grande morsel might also come my way—then, presto! My purr will sound like music to accompany this lady and gentleman I sit close to, eh?"

*Chomp*
*Chomp*
*Chomp*

**"Shoooo, cat! Shoooo!"**

yelled the lady and gentleman.

So Pino moved on. But without a musical purr to accompany him.

# TRIP, CRASH, SPLASH!

"Just the notes I wanted to hear!
Bravo! Mmmmm . . . such spices,
what flavor! A fine stew . . .
Pino is eating like a king!"

Chomp
Chomp
Chomp

Pino, Pino, did you find
That special meal—the better kind?
Sampling tidbits, spiced to perfection,
But are they served with affection?

OOO!!!"

Tired and lonely, sticky and cold,
Pino stopped and looked up at the moon.
"I have tasted the finest in cuisine,
yet my purr is more pitiful than ever.
Luna, just look at you—so full and
content. Pino would like to be, too."

"Luna, am I imagining things?
  You are beginning to look
  a little like someone I know."
Pino lifted his nose and sniffed the air.
"MMMMmmmmmmm.
  And here is an aroma I know, too—

"an aroma so sweet my tail
and whiskers are curling!

"An aroma spiced to

*ppppuuuuuuuuuurrrrrrrfection*

can only be . . .

"the Signora's pasta!

The only meal that fills my heart
and makes me purr like the
best-loved cat in all of Rome!"

Pino, Pino, you are home,
The most loving place in all of Rome.
Now you know. It is true—
Signora's pasta, the meal for you!

Purr

Purr

Purr

Purr